THE THIEVES OF PECK'S POCKET

Teryl Euvremer

Crown Publishers, Inc.
New York

To Emma

Published by Crown Publishers, Inc., a Random House company,
225 Park Avenue South, New York, New York 10003
CROWN is a trademark of Crown Publishers, Inc.
Manufactured in Hong Kong

Library of Congress Cataloging-in-Publication Data
Euvremer, Teryl. The thieves of Peck's Pocket / Teryl Euvremer.
Summary: Three greedy thieves who have robbed their town bare get
their just desserts when a magical flowering plant traps them in their
home. [1. Robbers and outlaws—Fiction.]   I. Title.
PZ7.E8735Th   1990   [E]—dc20   89-23845
ISBN 0-517-57537-X
       0-517-57538-8 (lib. bdg.)

10 9 8 7 6 5 4 3 2 1

First Edition

What a crafty pack of thieves were Croc, Brac, and Stoc! Instead of lying low in a ramshackle hideout like ordinary bandits, they lived smack in the middle of town.

All day long the honest folk of Peck's Pocket passed the tidy house where Croc, Brac, and Stoc slept with curtains tightly drawn.

At night, while the town slumbered, out they
popped…and the burgling began.

Greedy Croc stole anything that he could crack
between his teeth. Sneaking into a darkened pantry,
he'd snaffle up the dill pickles, gingersnaps, and ham
on the bone. A smear of goose fat on the hinges kept
the door from squealing as he made his exit.

Brac fancied bric-a-brac. She pilfered the porcelain
shepherdesses that mind candlesticks on mantlepieces,
purloined postcard collections, helped herself to
heirloom rings and thimbles, swept the knickknacks
off lamp stands, the trinkets off shelves...

Stoc's game was heavy furniture. Shifting a davenport
or grand piano across town was as easy for that
hefty housebreaker as moving checkers across a board.

After he'd emptied the parlor and the dining
room, he'd tiptoe upstairs.

Snug under thick eiderdowns, the good townsfolk
lay fast asleep. Delicately Stoc would lift them, one
by one, and set them on the floor. Beds, bolsters, and
all would vanish out of a window.

Nothing would be left. No, not a thing. And before the first rooster had crowed, Croc, Brac, and Stoc would have flown the coop.

The time came when every house in Peck's Pocket had been stripped bare. Townsfolk discussed this uncomfortable situation while Croc, Brac, and Stoc curled up in cramped quarters.

The three criminals continued to prowl, but the pickings were slim.

One moonless night the shifty trio were feeling their way down a dark alley when Brac's searching fingertips grazed something on a stoop and set it rocking. Her low yap was a signal to the others.

"What have you got?" whispered Stoc.

"Search me!" murmured Brac.

"Let's take it home," said Croc.

And they did.

"It's only a plant," said Stoc.

"Might make a nice salad," suggested Croc.

"Or keep off fleas," grunted Stoc. "Those round things look poisonous."

"There's a label," Brac said, and read aloud: "*Captigonia scoundrelis*…Gives me goose flesh. Imagine! Just a sprout, and already budding! It would be criminal to eat it, at least before it flowers."

"Our house is full to bursting!" protested Stoc.

"Let's plant it!" said Croc and Brac.

Croc dug a hole and tapped the *Captigonia scoundrelis* lightly into place. The earth felt pleasant between his claws, like noodle dough.

"If it bears fruit, I'll make jam," he said.

Brac pulled some weeds and hoed the ground around it.

"I wonder what color the flowers will be," she said.. "I'll bet these buds open up when the sun hits them. If we go to bed now," she added, "we might miss the whole show."

Stoc yawned.

"Robbers don't grow flowers," he grumbled. But he grabbed a watering can and sprinkled the plant.

All that day the three crooks drank strong coffee
and played loud music to keep themselves awake. It
was a big disappointment when the *Captigonia
scoundrelis* didn't bloom. Croc, Brac, and Stoc went
to bed with the sun, like everyone else in town.

The three outlaws got into the habit of gardening in broad daylight. The *Peck's Pocket Crier* had no new thefts to report.

The *Captigonia* was thriving. Its buds were round-cheeked and glowing. When would they open?

Spring went by. Neighbors stopped to admire the unusual plant. Its tightly closed buds were as big as Stoc's fists.

Everyone in town could see that Croc, Brac, and Stoc had green thumbs. Who could have guessed that they also had sticky fingers? The three smug gardeners polished the *Captigonia*'s already shiny leaves. Passersby gaped at the splendid greenery.

"Tomorrow it will bloom," said Croc, Brac, and Stoc. "Take our word for it."

Then one day it did. At sunrise Croc, Brac, and Stoc looked out at the first brilliant blooms.

"I knew they would be purple," said Brac.

"What dazzling delectability!" Croc sighed. "What a luscious lollapalooza! What an absolute out-and-out eyeful!"

Stoc beamed. What more could one say? He dipped his nose between the leaves to take a sniff. Then his grin collapsed into a fanged frown.

"Don't tell me it stinks!" said Brac.

"It smells wonderful," said Stoc. "But I don't like the way those branches have grown since yesterday. They're so much taller. And thicker. They remind me of something..."

"Jail!" cried Croc.

"You muttonheads!" said Brac. "Just push the branches aside."

But they couldn't. Stoc's brawny biceps and Croc's crowbar were useless.

"We'll have to break out!" bellowed Stoc, flinging himself against the door. But the door wouldn't budge.

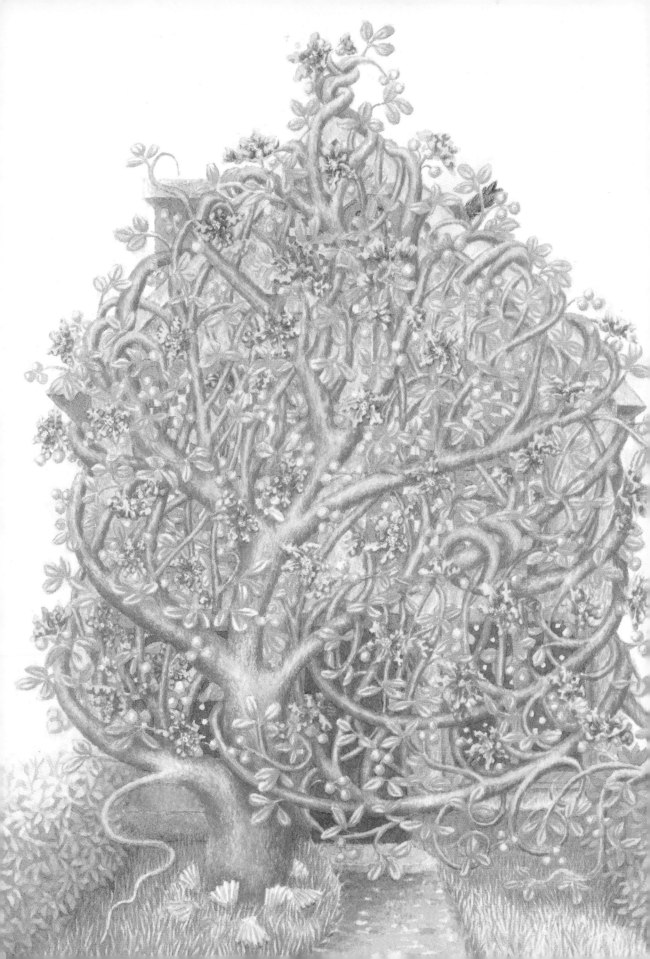

Frantically Croc, Brac, and Stoc clambered up their mountain of spoils, throwing open windows. Thick, flowering branches barred them all.

"Our goose is cooked," moaned Croc.

"Try the skylight," said Brac.

Stoc reached up between the rafters and yanked it open. The colossal *Captigonia* had spread across the roof, making a tight, green parcel of the house.

"Hack the plant down!" thundered Stoc.

"Not for all the mulligan stew in town," snapped Croc, looking lovingly at the flowers.

Brac rubbed her shins thoughtfully.

"Chop down the *Captigonia scoundrelis*?" she said. "Are you crazy? We grew it ourselves, from just a sprout. We hoed and weeded it; we polished its leaves! And *who* watered it every day?"

Stoc's ears turned a telltale red. The three poor devils sat on their thieving paws while the *Captigonia* flowers opened under the early sun.

A tiny sound broke the somber silence. A long, smooth shoot was scraping its way down the chimney flue. A tendril appeared, beckoning, like a crooked finger. The three sorry rogues skidded down the monstrous heap.

Then they shinnied up the green rope, sprang from the chimney, and made for the mountains.

On Peck's Pocket Bluff they stopped and looked back at the town. Its streets were bustling with activity. Their house, hidden under its mass of leaves and flowers, was beginning to attract attention.

They watched a crowd gather. The townsfolk pointed and came close to smell the blossoms. Children lifted the shiny leaves and peered in the windows. Suddenly the *Captigonia scoundrelis* reared back, revealing the front door.

Croc, Brac, and Stoc turned tail and ran.

Summer had passed. A wary moon watched the
infamous three sneak back into town.

The *Captigonia scoundrelis* still covered the ransacked house, but its shiny leaves had yellowed and begun to drop. Where glorious purple flowers had bloomed, round seed pods hung. When Brac snapped one off its brittle stem, it rattled. She pocketed it quickly.

Without a glance behind them, Croc, Brac, and Stoc left the town for good.

Far from there, three gardeners live off the fat of the land. One of them is called Croc. His garden overflows with magnificent vegetables. Any passerby can fill his basket with them, and welcome. Croc always seems to have more than he needs.

The second gardener is Stoc. In his orchard the trees bend low, so that each succulent fruit is within easy grasp. Some folks don't like to go to the trouble of picking, so Stoc always leaves a few bushels by the roadside.

Brac's flower garden never stops blooming, all the year round. But the best time to go and see it is in the middle of summer when the *Captigonia scoundrelis* is in bloom with shiny leaves and fragrant purple blossoms. It towers above Brac's cottage, reaching for the clouds.

To everyone who admires her flowers, Brac is
quick to say:
"Pick them. Pick them all!"

Croc, Brac, and Stoc are still fast friends. They drop in on one another every day, and sometimes even at night. Just like old times!